She's VERY excited.

I am, too!

Well, we ARE in
a pretty great book.....

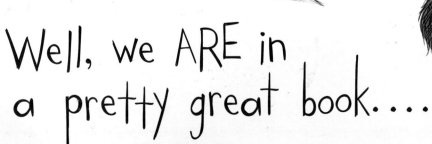

For Tara Lazar. Thanks for the push.
—T.S.

For Sara
—D.M.

Text copyright © 2018 by Tammi Sauer
Jacket art and interior illustrations copyright © 2018 by David Mottram

All rights reserved. Published in the United States by Doubleday,
an imprint of Random House Children's Books,
a division of Penguin Random House LLC, New York.

Doubleday and the colophon are registered trademarks of Penguin Random House LLC.

Visit us on the Web! randomhousekids.com

Educators and librarians, for a variety of teaching tools,
visit us at RHTeachersLibrarians.com

Library of Congress Cataloging-in-Publication Data is available upon request.
ISBN 978-1-5247-1929-6 (trade) — ISBN 978-1-5247-1930-2 (lib. bdg.) —
ISBN 978-1-5247-1932-6 (ebook)

Book design by Nicole de las Heras

MANUFACTURED IN CHINA
10 9 8 7 6 5 4 3 2 1
First Edition

WORDY BiRDY

Written by
Tammi Sauer

Illustrated by
Dave Mottram

Doubleday Books
for Young Readers

Meet Wordy Birdy.
Wordy Birdy has *lots* to say.
It starts the moment she wakes up.
See?

Sometimes Wordy Birdy talks about what she likes.

I like spaghetti and unicorns and library books and polka dots and standing on my head and...

Sometimes she talks about what she doesn't like.

I don't like tall grass or turtlenecks or long lines or tuna salad or losing my balloon or...

Sometimes she just asks questions.

But she never stops talking long enough to get the answers.
Wordy Birdy is not the world's best listener.

Oh, puh-/ease.

Are we talking about the same bird here?

Okay. Okay. Wordy Birdy is *terrible* at listening.

That's more like it.

She never listens to anybody.

Even when she should.

One day, Wordy Birdy takes a walk into the deep woods.
Naturally, she has plenty to say.

Before long, Squirrel zips in front of Wordy Birdy.

STOP! Don't go any farther!

Does Wordy Birdy listen?

Soon, Rabbit dashes onto the scene.

Go back while you still can!

Does Wordy Birdy listen?

Then Raccoon gives a piece of advice.

Does Wordy Birdy listen?

Do Squirrel, Rabbit, and Raccoon just leave Wordy Birdy there?

And Wordy Birdy?

Then Wordy Birdy says thank you the best way she knows how.

I love you guys! Like, I really, really, really love you. Seriously! I love you more than spaghetti and unicorns and...

Wordy Birdy still likes to talk. *A lot.*
See?

Good night, sunset.
Good night, orange sky.
Good night, purple—
Ooh! Good night, you.

But sometimes . . .

. . . she likes to listen, too.